The Berenstain Bears® VISIT FUN PARK

Stan & Jan Berenstain

A GOLDEN BOOK · NEW YORK

Western Publishing Company, Inc., Racine, Wisconsin 53404

ISBN: 0-307-23175-5

Look, cubs! Look!
Look, my dear!
Come and see
what I have here!

The supermarket
is giving away
Fun Park tickets
to shoppers today!

Oh, boy! Free tickets
for every ride!
Merry-Go-Round, Thunderbolt,
and Water Slide!

Into the car!

We are on our way!

We shall visit

Fun Park today!

This place is great!
It looks like fun!

FUN PARK

For fun, my son,
it's number one!

How about that ride?

It goes through water!

That ride's a bit

too wet, my daughter.

Now there's a ride *I*
was thinking of,
the ride that's called
the Tunnel of Love.

Remember, my dear?
We rode that ride
when you were a groom
and I was a bride.

9

Come. I have another
ride in mind.
A ride of a very
different kind.

A ride I rode
when, as a lad,
I came to Fun Park
with *my* dad.

I see a good ride,
Papa Bear.
Let's go on that one
over there.

The Merry-Go-Round?

It's much too boring.

I'd fall asleep.

I'd soon be snoring!

But, we're supposed
to be having fun!
And so far, Papa,
we've had none!

This ride you rode
when you were a lad—
will we ride it soon?
Please tell us, Dad!

It's up ahead!
My son, this ride
will be the best
you've ever tried!

And there it is!
Thunderbolt is its name.
Thunderbolt
is why we came!

That ride looks
very scary, Dad.

You'll love it, son.
Just trust your dad.

19

And years from now
when you are grown
and have some cubs
of your own—

The Thunderbolt,
without a doubt,
is the ride you'll tell
your cubs about!

This way please.
Strap yourselves in.
The Thunderbolt ride
is about to begin.

The cubs enjoyed it.

Mama did, too.

But how about Papa?

What did he do?

Brave Papa Bear
hollered so loud,
you could hear him above
the roar of the crowd.

Y-E-E-E-E-O-O-O-O

After the ride,

poor Papa was quaking.

He sat on a bench

to try to stop shaking.

But, Papa—
Didn't you ride it
when you were a lad
when you came here
with your dad?

Yes, son, I did.
But, now I can see
I'm just not the lad
I used to be.

29

So the cubs took some tickets
and headed for fun.
Their day of rides
had just begun.

Then Mama remembered
what *she* had thought of.
She led Papa off
to the Tunnel of Love.